Dear Parent:
Your child's love of reading starts here!

Every child learns to read in a different way and at his or her own speed. Some go back and forth between reading levels and read favorite books again and again. Others read through each level in order. You can help your young reader improve and become more confident by encouraging his or her own interests and abilities. From books your child reads with you to the first books he or she reads alone, there are I Can Read Books for every stage of reading:

SHARED READING
Basic language, word repetition, and whimsical illustrations, ideal for sharing with your emergent reader

BEGINNING READING
Short sentences, familiar words, and simple concepts for children eager to read on their own

READING WITH HELP
Engaging stories, longer sentences, and language play for developing readers

READING ALONE
Complex plots, challenging vocabulary, and high-interest topics for the independent reader

ADVANCED READING
Short paragraphs, chapters, and exciting themes for the perfect bridge to chapter books

I Can Read Books have introduced children to the joy of reading since 1957. Featuring award-winning authors and illustrators and a fabulous cast of beloved characters, I Can Read Books set the standard for beginning readers.

A lifetime of discovery begins with the magical words "I Can Read!"

Visit www.icanread.com for information
on enriching your child's reading experience.

I Can Read Book® is a trademark of HarperCollins Publishers.

Spider-Man Versus the Scorpion
© 2010 Marvel Entertainment, Inc., and its subsidiaries. MARVEL, all related characters and the distinctive likenesses thereof:
™ and © 2010 Marvel Entertainment, Inc., and its subsidiaries. Licensed by Marvel Characters B.V. www.marvel.com. All rights
reserved. Printed in the United States of America. No part of this book may be used or reproduced in any manner whatsoever without
written permission except in the case of brief quotations embodied in critical articles and reviews. For information address Harper
Collins Children's Books, a division of HarperCollins Publishers, 10 East 53rd Street, New York, NY 10022.
www.icanread.com

Library of Congress catalog card number: 2009935251
ISBN 978-0-06-162623-4
Typography by Joe Merkel

11   12   13   LP/WOR   10 9 8 7 6 5   ❖   First Edition

I Can Read! READING 2 WITH HELP

SPIDER-SENSE SPIDER-MAN®

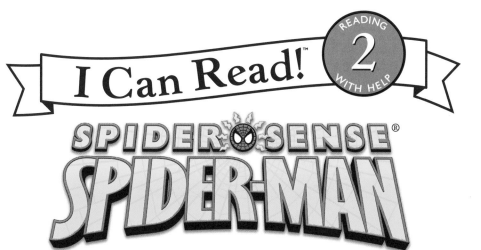

Spider-Man Versus the Scorpion

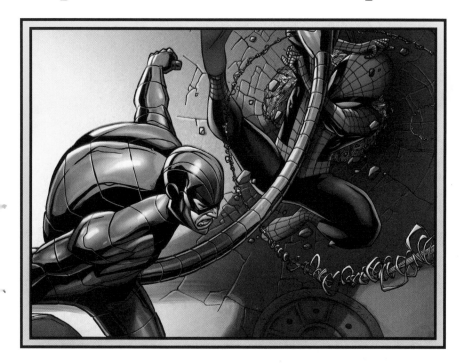

by Susan Hill
pictures by Andie Tong
colors by Jeremy Roberts

HARPER
An Imprint of HarperCollinsPublishers

PETER PARKER

Peter is a very good student.

LIZ ALLEN

He likes to study with his friend Liz.

THE SCORPION

Scorpion is Spider-Man's old foe.
But this time, Scorpion has some new tricks!

SPIDER-MAN

Liz doesn't know Peter's secret.
Peter Parker is also Spider-Man!

"Life is good!" said Peter Parker.
"School's out for the day,
I sold some pictures to the *Bugle*,
and I'm on my way to meet Liz Allen
at the library."

"I've got one hour," Peter said
as he ran down the steps
to the subway.
"That's plenty of time to get
to the library."

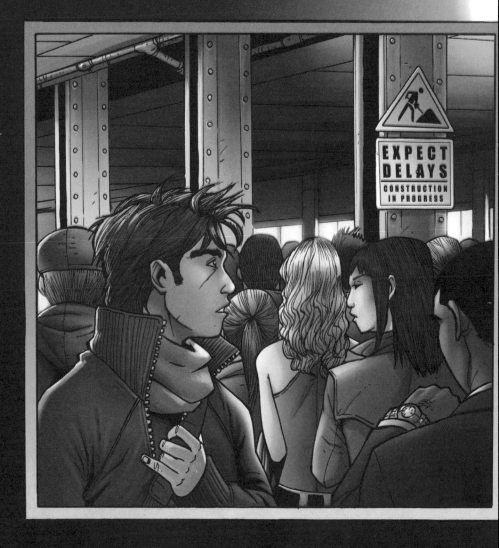

"Oh, no!" Peter grumbled.

The trains were delayed.

"I'll never get there in time!"

he said.

Then Peter remembered something.
"Peter Parker might not get there
in time, but Spider-Man will!"
he said.
He put on his Super Hero costume.

Spider-Man shot a web
and swung away.
"Now nothing can stop me!"
he said.

Then Peter saw a strange person

crashing his way out of a bank.

"Nothing can stop me

except a bad guy with a tail.

Hey, Scorpion!" Spidey called.

"Back for a rematch?"

Scorpion swung around.

"It's my lucky day!" he cried.

"First I stole all this money,

and now I get to squash Spider-Man!"

"Give back the money, Scorpy,"
said Spider-Man.
"And then I'll be on my merry way
to the library."

13

"Library?" said Scorpion.

"Did I say library?" said Spidey.

"I meant secret hideout."

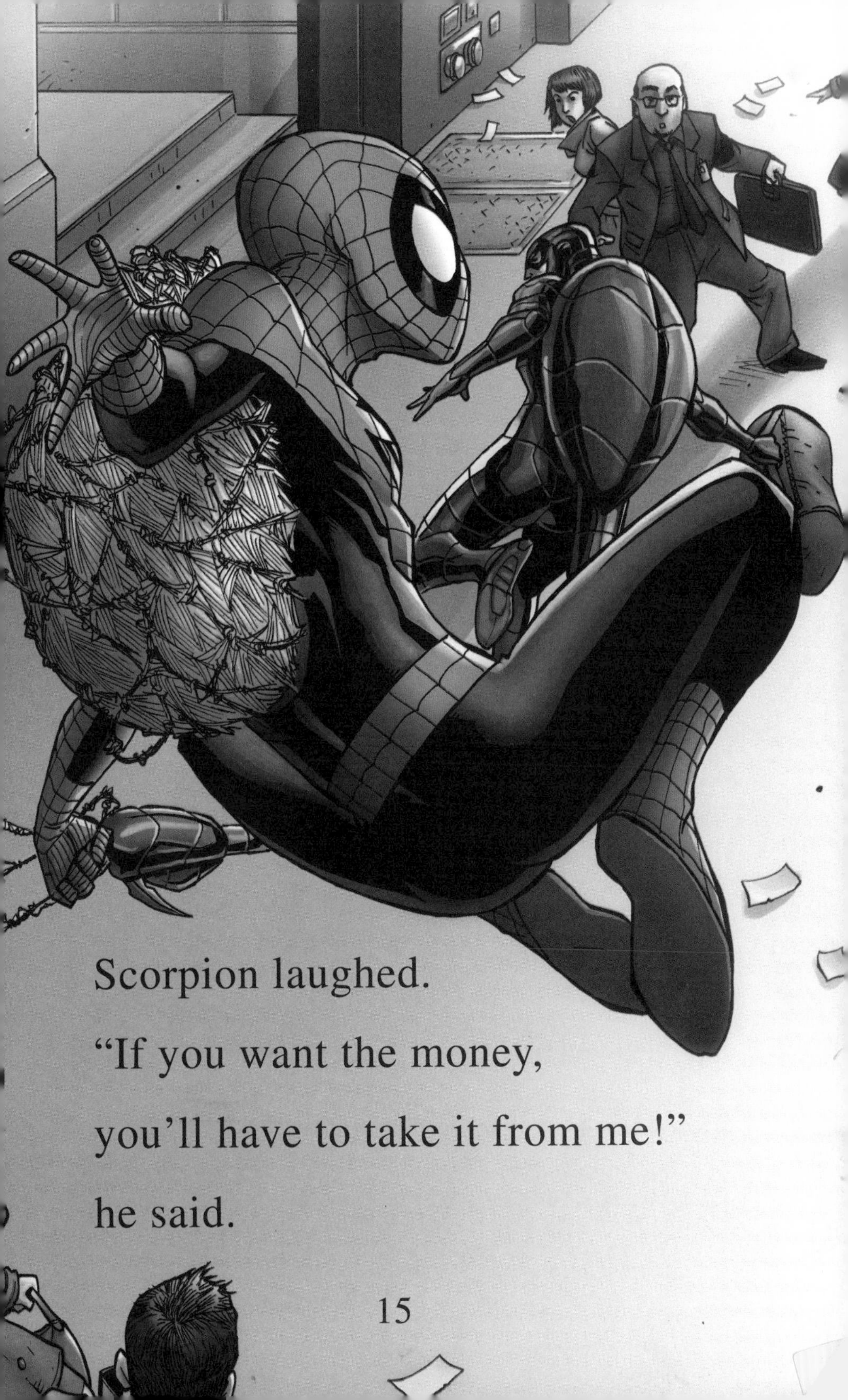

Scorpion laughed.
"If you want the money,
you'll have to take it from me!"
he said.

Spider-Man shot a web at Scorpion.
"Don't worry, Scorpion,
this won't sting," said Spidey.

But Scorpion was too strong
for Spider-Man's webs.
He broke free and ran after Spidey.
"Don't you know that scorpions
eat spiders for lunch?" said the villain.

"I've made some changes
since our last battle," Scorpion said.
Scorpion lashed out his strong tail
and knocked Spidey to the ground.
"That new tail makes him stronger
than I am," Spidey said to himself.
"This time, instead of beating
Scorpion with spider-strength,
I'll have to beat him
with spider smarts!"

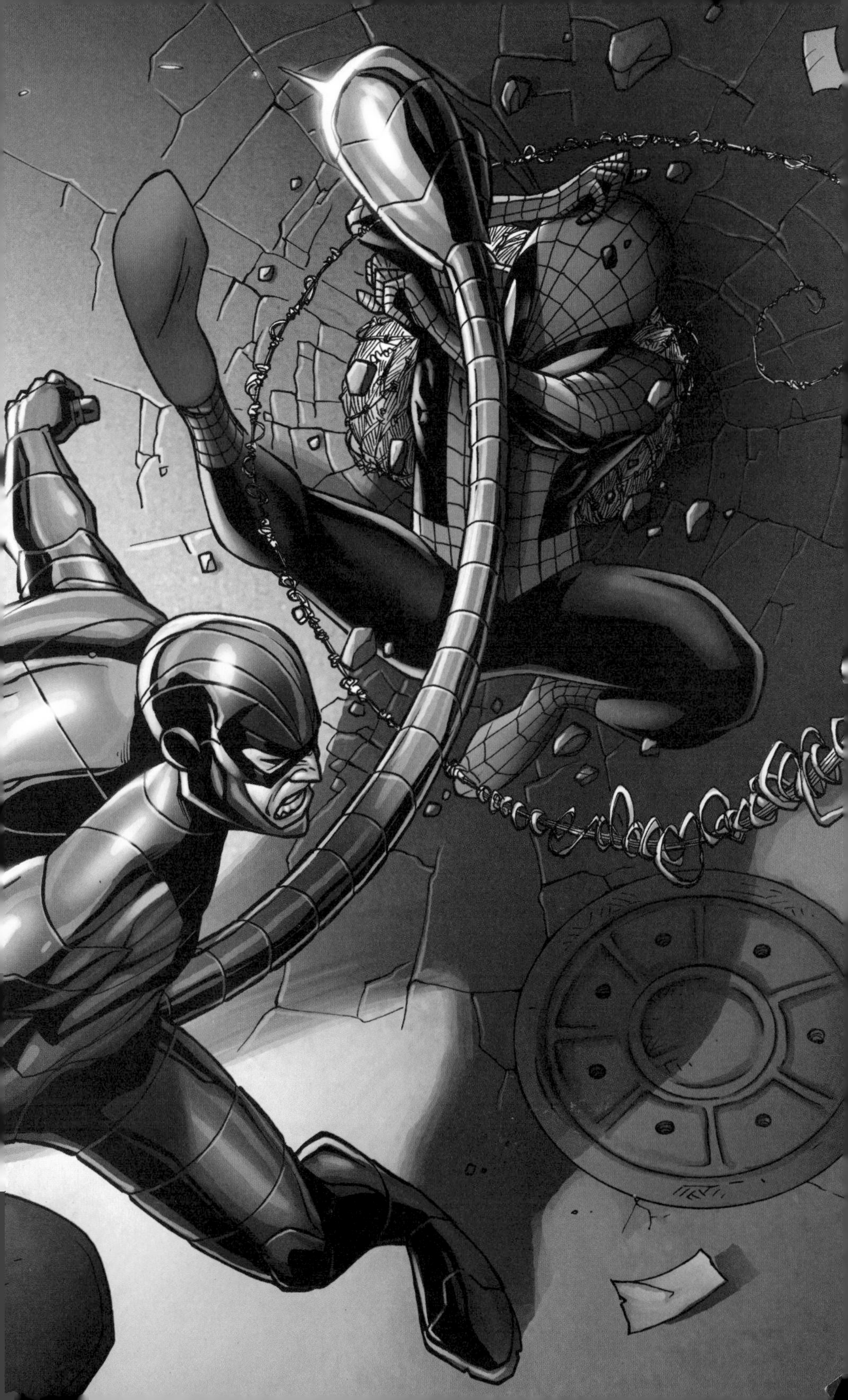

Scorpion lashed his tail up and down.

Spider-Man jumped over it.

"Aren't we a little old for games

like jump rope?" said Spidey.

"Game over," said Scorpion.

Scorpion raised his tail high.

He crashed it down on Spider-Man.

"I knew I could squash you like a bug," said Scorpion.

He turned to leave.

Spidey lay flat on the ground.

Spidey leaped up suddenly.

He grabbed Scorpion's tail.

"This spider was playing possum,"

said Spider-Man.

"Hang on, Scorpy," said Spider-Man.
"You might feel a little pinch!"
Spider-Man yanked the tail
from Scorpion's body.

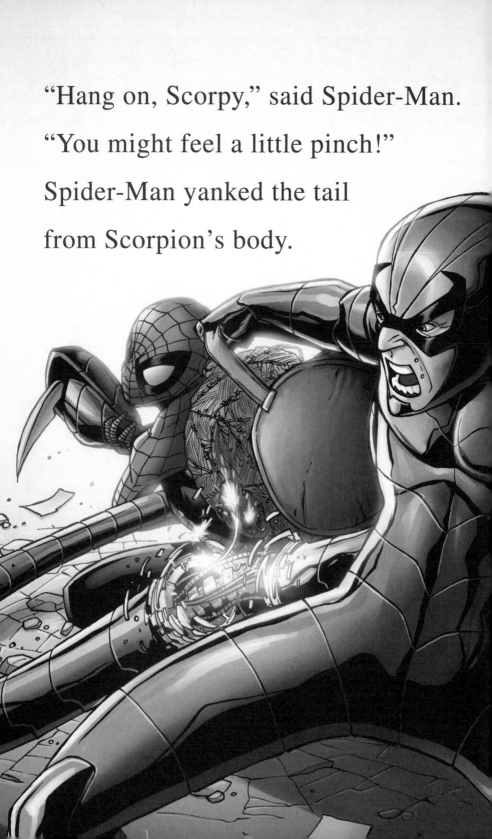

"My power is gone!"

yelled Scorpion.

Spider-Man wrapped the tail

around Scorpion.

"Looks like we've reached the

tail end of this battle!" he said.

"So long, Scorpion," said Spider-Man
as he dropped off the villain
with the police.

"Time to catch the express line,"
said Spider-Man.

He jumped on top of a passing train
and rode it to the library.

Quickly Spider-Man changed.

He hid his costume

and ran up the library steps.

"I'm right on time," he said.

Peter found Liz Allen.

"I made it, Liz!" said Peter.

"You might say it took superpowers
to get here on time," he added.

"But Peter, you're super late!"

said Liz.

"Our study date was yesterday."

Peter hung his head.

"Just my luck,"

Peter said to himself quietly.

"Spider-Man saves the day,

but Peter Parker messes it up."

"Do you have time to study now?" asked Liz.

Peter smiled.

"All the time in the world," he said.